On Wimbledon Common, under the ground in their Burrow, live

The WOMBLES

Beautiful Boating Weather

Adapted by Elisabeth Beresford

from the Wombles television series produced by CINAR and UFTP

Hodder
Children's
Books

a division of Hodder Headline plc

The young Wombles had been working so hard clearing up the rubbish on the Common that Great Uncle Bulgaria and Tobermory decided they should have a treat. So they called them all into Great Uncle Bulgaria's study.

"How would you like a day off?" he said.

Everybody had their own idea about what they would like to do most. Orinoco wanted to have a long snooze with plenty of Madame Cholet's cakes to keep him going. Tomsk imagined himself taking part in the Olympic Games and Alderney said,

"Let's have a picnic on the lake!"

Bungo and Tomsk thought it was a great idea, but Stepney kept quiet.

All the others collected an enormous hamper of food from Madame Cholet, some fishing rods, books and music, and then off they went in the Womble boat.

Alderney got out a fishing line and they all started eating the picnic, while Shansi played some music.

One gooseberry tart was left. Orinoco and Bungo began to squabble over it and they both tugged at it at the same time.

The boat started to rock up and down and the next moment the tart AND the oars fell into the water with a splash.

"Now you've done it!" said Wellington. "We're stuck in the middle of the lake!"

Back at the Burrow, Great Uncle Bulgaria was doing the crossword and enjoying a bit of peace and quiet when Stepney came up with his squeaky barrow.

"Why aren't you with the others?" asked Great Uncle Bulgaria.

"Well, the truth is I'm not very keen on boats and water," mumbled Stepney. "I think I'll just go on clearing up . . ." And off he squeaked.

Meanwhile the others were trying
to get back to the shore.
 They made a tower of
Wombles with Tomsk on the top.
He made a grab for a branch of
the tree which hung over the lake.
But he missed it and the next
moment he was hanging
from the branch by
his life jacket!

Stepney was pushing his squeaking barrow down to the lake, but it was squeaking so loudly he didn't hear what was going on. Bungo was making a grab for one of the oars while everybody else was hanging on to him.

Bungo just managed to get it, but rowing with only one oar made the boat go round and round in circles.

Then Wellington had another of his great ideas . . .

Shansi had to sit on one end of the oar - which was balanced across Orinoco's fat stomach - and all the others had to hang on to the other end.

"One, two, three . . ." shouted Wellington, and they all pulled on their end of the oar. The next moment Shansi was flying through the air!

"Wheeeee!" she cried.

Everybody else
shut their eyes, but Shansi
wasn't worried. She landed
on the branch next to Tomsk.

"I wonder what they're all up to,"
Stepney was saying to himself as he
plodded on his way, tidying up an
old rubber ring as he went.

Down in the boat, Alderney, Wellington and Bungo were holding out the picnic blanket underneath the tree.

"Jump, Tomsk!" shouted Alderney.

Tomsk did as he was told - with his eyes shut - but instead of landing on the blanket, he fell straight onto Orinoco's tummy and then bounced off it.

Orinoco woke up.

Shansi jumped next, just as Stepney came into sight and everybody shouted:
    "Heeelp, Stepney, heeelp."
    "Sounds as if they're in trouble," he said to himself, as he ran towards them with his barrow.

Stepney knew how he could rescue them. He took all the rubbish he had picked up and made it into a raft. Then he tied one end of a piece of rope to his barrow and the other end to the raft. And then he took a very deep breath.

"It's only water," he said to himself, "nothing to be afraid of!"

He put on the rubber ring, stepped onto the raft and paddled himself out to the boat.

The others were so pleased to see him. Stepney climbed into the boat and then pulled on the rope to take them back to the shore.

"Well, young Stepney," said Great Uncle Bulgaria, back at the Burrow, "did you enjoy your first boat trip?"

"Not a lot," said Stepney. "I still think Wombles should stay on dry ground!"

"Perhaps you're right," agreed Great Uncle Bulgaria. "Now come and have your supper. You deserve it!"

Photographs and original artwork,
courtesy of FilmFair Ltd.
a subsidiary of CINAR Films Inc.

ISBN 0 340 73583 X

10 9 8 7 6 5 4 3 2 1

A catalogue record for this book
is available from the British Library.

Printed in Great Britain

Hodder Children's Books
a division of Hodder Headline plc
338 Euston Road, London NW1 3BH